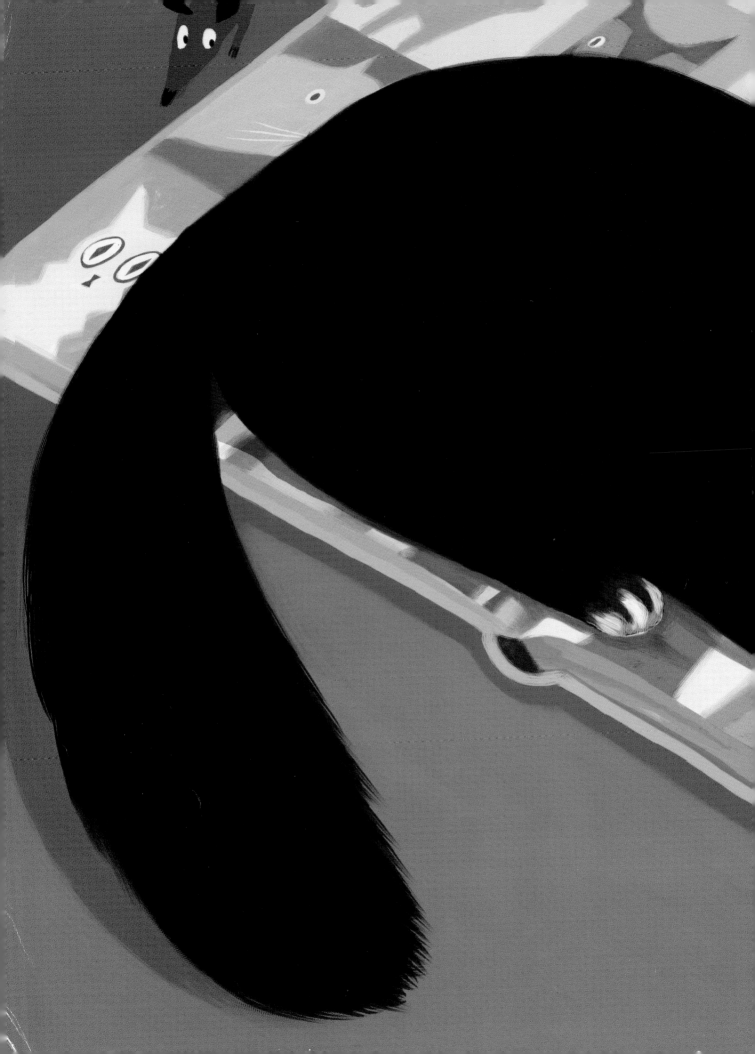

Nobody's Nosier Than a Cat

By Susan Campbell Bartoletti
Illustrations by Beppe Giacobbe

Hyperion Books
for Children
New York

First Edition
1 3 5 7 9 10 8 6 4 2

This book is set in Phoenix Chunky.
The art for this book was created on a Macintosh G4
computer using Fractal Design Painter and Adobe Photoshop.
Library of Congress Cataloging-in-Publication Data on file.
ISBN 0-7868-1614-7

Printed in Singapore

Visit www.hyperionchildrensbooks.com

To my brother Dan
—S.C.B.

To Marco, Lila, and Giacomo
—B.G.

Nobody's
NOSiER
than a cat—

a moon-eyed cat,

a night-watch cat.

Nobody's **dozier** than a cat—

a sun-spot,

Queen-of-the-Couch cat.

Nobody's trickier than a cat—

a
top-
spot
cat,

an aCrobAT cat.

Nobody's *lickier* than a cat—

a rough-tongue, wash-all-over cat.

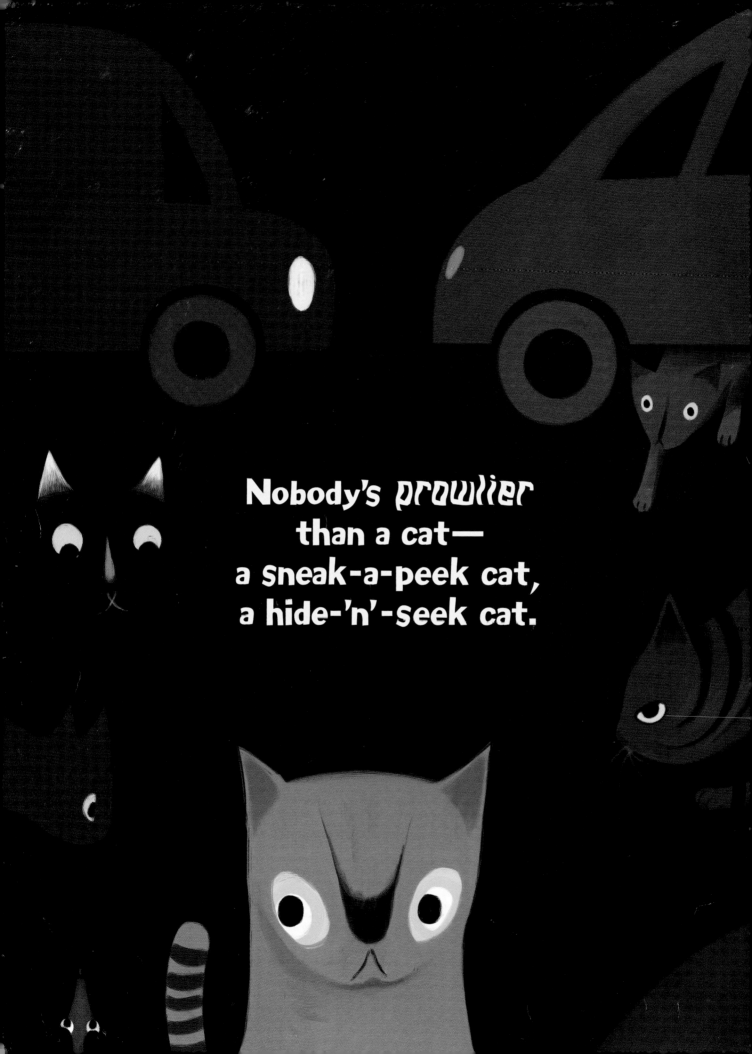

Nobody's *prowlier*
than a cat—
a sneak-a-peek cat,
a hide-'n'-seek cat.

Nobody's GROWLIER than a cat—

a hunchback,

tough-'hood, stand-back cat!

Nobody's naughtier than a cat—

a tear-the-chair cat, a garbage-can cat.

Nobody's *spookier* than a cat—

a
tip-
toe
cat,

a
shadow
cat.

a tail-
trail,
skitty-
scat,
catnip-
clown
cat.

Nobody's **HOAXIER** than a cat—
an in-a-sack cat, a sneak-attack cat.

Nobody's **coaxier** than a cat—
a round-the-leg, in-your-face,
feed-me-NOW cat.

Nobody's sheddier
than a cat—

a puff-of-fluff cat,

a scratch-that-flea cat.

Nobody's **steadier** than a cat—
a ledge-walker, bird-stalker,
pounce-trounce cat.

Nobody's *mopier* than a cat— a slouchy-grouch cat, a lonely-soul cat.

Nobody's **SOAPIER** than a cat—

an ears-flat, skinny-matte, catch-that cat!

Nobody's posier than a cat—

a windowsill cat, a daze-'n'-gaze cat.

Nobody's *cozier*
than a cat—

a purred-up,

curled-up,

take-a-nap cat.

Needing-a-lap . . .

My lap.

My cat.